Squishy Taylor is published by
Picture Window Books,
A Capstone Imprint
1710 Roe Crest Drive
North Mankato, Minnesota 56003
www.mycapstone.com

Squishy Taylor and the Mess-Makers
Text copyright © 2016 Ailsa Wild
Illustration copyright © 2016 Ben Wood
Series design copyright © 2016 Hardie Grant Egmont
First published in Australia by Hardie Grant Egmont 2016

Published in American English in 2018 by Picture Window Books

Library of Congress Cataloging-in-Publication Data
is on file with the Library of Congress.

ISBN: 978-1-5158-1973-8 (paperback)
ISBN: 978-1-5158-1977-6 (reflowable epub)

Summary: Squishy's favorite movie star is filming on their street,
right next door! But could Carmeline Clancy really be as naughty as
the media says? Only Squishy, Vee, and Jessie can solve
this mystery . . .

Printed in China.
010735S18

and the
Mess-Makers

Ailsa Wild

with art by BEN WOOD

PICTURE WINDOW BOOKS
a capstone imprint

For Odette and Zephyr —
my own bonus family.
Together you helped me invent Baby.
— Ailsa

For my little mess-makers,
Wombat and Bilby.
— Ben

Chapter One

I hold my breath as she grabs a ledge of rock with one hand. She **grips tight**, her knuckles pale. The sky behind her is so bright, it's scary. She slips a little, and her fingers slide back toward the edge.

There is a blur of rope and rock and a **thump** as her shoulder hits the cliff.

Carmeline Clancy's familiar laugh rings out, and I let my breath out in a

whoosh. I'm watching her on the big TV screen in the lobby of Rockers, our rock climbing center. I've seen these clips hundreds of times on YouTube. I loved Carmeline Clancy before she got famous.

Carmeline is from Colorado. She's the youngest person ever to climb up **Lincoln's Terror**, one of the hardest climbs in the universe. She straps her camera to her helmet, so you can watch the crazy stuff she does as she does it. Her YouTube channel is the best.

Usually the videos playing in the rock climbing center are of grown-up men. Not today, though. Carmeline Clancy is in the news because she's making a movie and doing **all her own stunts**.

They're filming some of the scenes right here in our city this week.

I want to *be* Carmeline Clancy. Or maybe I just want to hang out with her forever. I can't decide which.

I turn to look at my bonus sister Vee as the next video clip begins. I call her my bonus sister, because she was an awesome gift I got when I moved in with my dad. Vee is fun.

"I'm going to find Carmeline Clancy tomorrow and get her to sign my rock climbing top," I say.

"I'm going to make friends with her, and then I'll get to be in the movie," Vee says.

"She's going to make me a special stunt person in *zillions* of her movies,"

I say. **"Squishy Taylor, stunt-climber!"** I say in a TV announcer voice.

That's me, Squishy Taylor. My real name is Sita, after my grandmother, but Squishy is a special nickname my parents gave me when I was little.

Vee grins and says, "I'm going to Colorado to take her title as the youngest person to climb Lincoln's Terror."

We both laugh. "You can't even climb the **Gargoyle's Escape** yet," I say.

The Gargoyle's Escape is the hardest climb at Rockers. I can only do the first half of it. Vee is a little bit better than I am but not much, and she's been rock climbing for a lot longer than me. I only started when I moved in with her after my dad and her mom got married and had Baby.

A voice-over comes on the TV: "*Rock climbing child superstar Carmeline Clancy arrived in town yesterday, and she is already making waves —*"

"All right, you two," says someone behind us. "Giddy-up!" It's Alice, Vee's mom, coming out with our bags. Baby is asleep in the sling with his big head under her chin. Alice stands right in front of the screen so we can't see.

"Let's go," she says, turning our shoulders toward the door.

"Hang on," I say, straining to keep looking at the screen. The announcer is saying something in a serious tone, but I can't make out the words.

Alice turns around, but it's too late. The voice-over has stopped and now they're playing one of Carmeline's more **awesome falls.**

"Come on, Squishy," Alice says.

"They were talking about Carmeline Clancy," I say.

"Of course they were," says Alice, like the only thing anyone *ever* talks about is Carmeline Clancy. Which is kind of true in our house.

On the way home, Vee and I do some **upside-down scissor-kicks** from the bus handles. Vee can do more than I can, but I do better flips because I

practice on the monkey bars at school. Vee is in the grade above me. Those kids don't do monkey bars anymore. Vee says she doesn't care, but I'd care if I were her.

Alice hides her face in Baby's shoulder, pretending to be scared as I land from a flip. She looks up and says, "You just spent **two hours rock climbing.** Aren't you totally exhausted?"

"No!" we say and both jump upside down again.

"Well, I'm just going to pretend you don't belong to me, OK?"

I say, "OK, Alice!"

Vee says, "OK, Mom."

Vee's black ponytail swings in time with the swaying bus. My ponytail is too much of a **big curling tangle** to actually swing, but I like how it feels dangling off my head.

The bus stops four doors down from our building, opposite a big hotel. The hotel has shiny brass luggage carts and an outdoor carpet. There are even men in **fancy suits** just standing around waiting to be nice to people.

We cross the street at the light, toward the hotel, and Vee elbows me and points. A **scraggly gray puppy** is sitting next to one of the men. It's skinny and is looking up with soft, sad brown eyes. The man kicks it — not hard but still a kick.

"Hey!" I say, because that was *mean*.

The puppy scampers away, limping. It stops behind a big tree in front of the hotel, and I run toward it. I want to pick it up and cuddle it and feed it. But something scares the puppy, and it bolts across the road where I can't follow.

"Come on, Squishy." Alice says and tugs my hand. I follow her toward our place even though I don't want to.

"I'm calling the pound," the Fancy Man says.

I turn around to glare at him for being so mean but then immediately forget all about it. Because someone is getting out of a taxi and heading into the hotel.

"It's Carmeline Clancy!" I say.

Chapter Two

"It was *not* Carmeline Clancy," Jessie says, packing up her violin music. Jessie is Vee's twin, my other bonus sister. Even though they look the same, they're opposites in lots and lots of ways.

"It was *too*. I saw her," I insist.

"You wish you saw her," Jessie says in her annoying older—kid voice.

"I *did* see her."

The twins are only five and a half months older than me, but Jessie acts more grown-up all the time.

"Can you guys give it a break?" Alice asks. She's kneeling on the floor, and Baby is trying to kick her in the face while she wrangles his dirty diaper off him. Usually on Saturday morning, Dad looks after Baby while Alice goes rock climbing. This weekend one of Dad's friends is sick, so he went over with some food. That's why Baby came to the gym.

Baby is starting to wrinkle up his face. I calculate that he'll start screaming in nine seconds. I start counting down: *Nine, eight, seven . . .*

"Can I Google where Carmeline's staying?" Jessie asks.

Six, five . . .

Alice says nothing.

"Please, Mom?" Jessie even brings the iPad over.

Four, three . . .

"No."

"Please?"

Two, one . . .

"**Waaaaaaah!**" Baby is super loud when he's annoyed.

Alice sits back on her heels. "I said *no*, Jessie. Please listen to me. I need to take care of Baby right now."

Jessie **sulks off** to our room. You would think Jessie wouldn't care where Carmeline Clancy was staying, because she never watches the clips with us. She says they're soooooo boring.

But Jessie's into facts. And she's into **being right.**

I wonder if I really did see Carmeline Clancy getting out of that taxi.

In our room, Vee is lying on her tummy on the top bunk, looking through the telescope.

"How's Not-Boring Lady?" I ask.

Not-Boring Lady works in the office right across the street from our window. We used to think she was boring because all she did was type. Then we found out she was the Chief of Special Secret Undercover Operations. Now she's kind of like our **own special police officer.** She says it's OK if we see her in this office because she does her top-secret work in another, bigger office.

"I'm not looking at Not-Boring Lady," Vee says in a **scrunched-face voice**. I realize the telescope is at a different angle than usual. Vee's looking down at the street in front of the hotel.

"Can you see her?" I ask.

"Not yet," Vee says. We both know we're talking about Carmeline Clancy without saying her name. Because that's how much we care.

"You haven't seen her because she's not there," Jessie says. Jessie is putting her things away in neat rows in her drawers.

I get to Vee's bunk above mine with a **split-legged-upside-down-lift** and nudge her aside to look through the telescope. The view is totally different from up here. Usually I look from my bunk, which is in the middle. It looks directly across to Not-Boring Lady's office. From Jessie's bunk below mine, the telescope looks up at the stars. That's perfect, because Jessie is such an astronomy-head.

"How good is that tree?" Vee says. It's the tree the puppy hid behind. I've never really paid attention to the tree, but from here I can see that it's enormous, with wide, spreading branches reaching to the hotel wall. I shift the telescope to check out the rest of the tree. It would be a solid tree to climb.

When the telescope reaches the bottom of the trunk, I notice the puppy is back. The telescope is so good, I can see his beautiful eyes and the rib bones under his fur. He looks **trembly and sad.**

I wonder if Carmeline Clancy will come out again soon. I wonder if the puppy will stay still this time.

I have an idea. "Let's go outside and play hopscotch," I say.

We haven't played hopscotch since we used it as a cover to stakeout a diamond smuggler.

Vee grins. **"Brilliant!"**

Jessie agrees to come too. I guess practicing your violin and cleaning your room get boring after a while, even if you're Jessie. She finds the chalk in a drawer, lined up beside pencils and markers. Vee tells Alice what we're doing, and we pile out the door.

The puppy is gone again, but maybe it will come back. And maybe we'll see Carmeline Clancy. We stroll up the street and draw our **hopscotch court** as close as we can to the hotel, in the shade of the big tree. One of the Fancy Men glares at us, but we stay far enough away that he can't say anything.

We play three and a quarter games before Carmeline Clancy steps out of the hotel. **It IS her. At our hotel.** She's even wearing that rock climbing sports top from the famous overhang video! I grab Vee's arm, and we stare at her. She's real. Right there **on our sidewalk.** My skin feels tingly, and my ears buzz.

Carmeline is walking with a woman who's not her mom. I've seen her mom on YouTube. This woman is really tall, with a stiff back and **zero smiles**. One of the Fancy Men gets a taxi for them.

I'm all ready to run up and say hello to Carmeline, except my heart is going really fast. For the first time in my life, **I don't know what to say**. I push back my shoulders. It doesn't matter, I'm going over anyway.

The Fancy Man is opening the taxi door. If I'm not quick, Carmeline will be gone, and I will have missed my chance. As I walk toward them, the woman turns around and meets my eye.

She gives me **the death look**. It says: "Don't even think about coming one step closer. We don't want to see you. We don't want to *think* about you."

I stumble to a stop. The woman turns around and follows Carmeline into the taxi.

I stare after it as it disappears down the street. The Fancy Man looks at me a little strangely, but I don't care.

"Who do you think that lady is?" Vee asks, coming up beside me.

"I have no idea," I say. "But she **certainly is scary.**"

Chapter Three

I lie on the living room floor to call my mom on Skype before bedtime.

"Hello there, my Squishy," Mom says. "How was rock climbing?" She remembers everything I do, even though she's too busy to talk for very long.

"Good. Hey, can a security guard be a lady who's not in uniform?"

Mom knows lots of things about security people. She works for the United Nations in Geneva, Switzerland. Her job title even has the word "security" in it.

Mom laughs. "Absolutely. Got a new career plan, Squisho?'

I shake my head. "No," I say. "I know who the lady with Carmeline Clancy is."

"I should have known this would be about Carmeline Clancy," Mom says.

"She's staying in the hotel next door,'" I tell her.

It's not exactly next door, but Mom is **used to me exaggerating**. She already knows all about the new movie from me Skyping her every night.

She gives us her **Mom-look** and says, "You're not trying to figure out a way to meet her, are you?" She raises her eyebrows. "If you're planning to break into that hotel, I'm going to have to get on the next plane —"

Alice walks over with Baby on her hip. "Don't put any **crazy ideas** in their heads, Devika!" She's smiling, but she's got a little

bit of a warning tone. "Say hello to this guy instead." Alice sets Baby down between the screen and me.

Baby tries to eat the screen. It makes us all laugh. Then it's time for Mom's next meeting, because it's daytime in Geneva.

"I love you, Squishy-sweet," Mom says. Then she looks at Baby and gives him **kissy-kissy-faces** until I hang up.

There's no news of Carmeline Clancy all day Sunday and Monday. I don't see the puppy again either. It's not until Monday night that Dad turns on the TV news to watch while he's cooking. I'm sitting at the counter, **sneaking some cheese.**

After all the bad news reports finish, the news anchor puts on a fake smile and says: "*Well, the city is under attack by one young whirlwind who has done thousands of dollars worth of damage to her hotel room. Critics say rock-climber-turned-movie-star Carmeline Clancy is a troublemaker who . . .*"

The report is showing images of the hotel on our street, then video of **Carmeline climbing**, then other shots of **Carmeline looking sulky**. The images flash on the screen quickly, one after another.

"*Carmeline Clancy's Official Tour Nanny spoke with our reporter.*" An image of the scary woman comes up. She looks even **taller and scarier** with her arms crossed and staring down the camera.

"*This is absolutely out of character for Carmeline*," the Nanny begins.

"Oh, she's the *Tour Nanny*," Vee says. The woman doesn't look like a nanny to me, but Vee doesn't seem to notice. "Do you think Carmeline Clancy came here without her mom?" Vee's so busy talking that we don't hear the last part of the news.

The news switches over to the weather report.

I think about Carmeline Clancy's awesome YouTube clips. I can't imagine her **destroying a hotel room.**

"It wasn't her," I say.

"How would you know?" Jessie asks.

"I've watched her for hours," I say. "She's always really careful. And tidy. She's probably your real twin, swapped with Vee at birth." This is a joke, but Jessie doesn't laugh. "Carmeline Clancy definitely didn't do it."

"But you **don't have evidence** to prove it," Jessie says.

I think about mom warning me not to break into the hotel. "I'll ask her," I say.

"You will *not*," Jessie says.

Vee pops up from behind the couch where she's been building towers for Baby to knock down. She's got a smile on her face. "How are we gonna meet her?" she asks.

"Dinner!" Dad interrupts. "Someone wake up Alice."

"I'm awake," Alice says, opening their bedroom door. She takes naps before dinner some afternoons, because Baby is teething and keeps her awake at night.

Alice puts on her serious voice as she fills everyone's plates with broccoli. "I was listening to the news in there," she says, "about your rock climbing friend."

"She's not our friend," Jessie says.

Alice waves the tongs. "Whatever. I really don't want you kids having such a disrespectful person as a role model. I'm happy that you'd rather be athletes than princesses —"

We all smirk at each other. Princesses are so first grade.

"But," Alice goes on, holding up the tongs like a stop sign, "even the most famous stunt doubles need to be respectful of other people's things."

I get what Alice is saying, but she's wrong about one very important thing. "Carmeline Clancy isn't a stunt *double*. That's what's so cool about her," I say. "She's doing her own stunts."

Vee grins at me. One day we're going to do our own stunts.

Later, Vee interrupts my Skype session with Mom to throw a piece of paper down on my lap. "Look what I found in the recycling," she says.

I'm annoyed, because Mom only has about three minutes to talk to me. Vee is **taking my precious time**. But I read the piece of paper anyway, because it's in front of me.

Dear Residents, it says. It's a letter to everyone in our apartment building explaining that the road will be closed for filming over the next two weeks. *Sorry for the inconvenience.*

I wave the letter at the screen. "They're closing the street for Carmeline Clancy's film," I explain to Mom.

"Which street?" she asks.

I squint at the little map at the bottom of the letter. **"It's the one at the back of our building!"**

Chapter Four

At school, my friends are all obsessed with how bad Carmeline Clancy is. You can kind of hear their parents in their voices as they say things like "I wouldn't be friends with someone like that," and "She shouldn't be allowed on TV," and "It's so rude." They sit and **have a little agreeing party** together. Everyone agrees with everyone else, and then they agree some more. Carmeline Clancy seems to get worse and worse as they talk.

I suggest playing ninja monkey tag, but no one hears. They're all having too nice a time judging Carmeline.

I get upset and go looking for Vee. But she's with the older kids who all do **snob—face** at me.

I go do flips off the monkey bars by myself. I even talk to some first-grade kids for a little while until the bell rings.

On the bus, my bonus sisters and I **squash into the same seat**. Jessie picks up one of the free newspapers and starts reading it. It sounds weird that a kid would read the paper, but it's actually normal for Jessie. She **rustles a page** and says, "Hey, you guys, look at this."

She slides the paper onto Vee's lap. The headline says: *PHOTOS OF CHILD STAR'S RUINED HOTEL ROOM LEAKED BY HOUSEKEEPING STAFF.*

Underneath, it says, *"Third night of chaos in a row,"* states secret source.

The pictures in the paper show a hotel room that **looks like a war zone.** Sheets are torn up, and there's food all over the floor. Sections of wallpaper have been ripped off the wall and are hanging down in flaps. It looks really bad.

Carmeline Clancy says she "didn't do it" but refuses to explain the situation, the newspaper says.

They say **"didn't do it"** like they are saying she's lying but without really saying it. That's what makes me the angriest about this article.

When we get off at our bus stop, the puppy is sitting by a side door of the hotel. His **fur looks a little shinier** than the last time I saw him. I want to run across the road and cuddle him, but by the time the lights have changed, **the puppy is gone.**

"Where is that poor child's mother?" Mom asks on Skype that night. She has on her **worried-Mom-face.** That makes me worried too.

"Probably in Geneva," I say, which makes Mom feel bad, even though I only said it to be funny.

"I mean, whose job is it to keep her safe?" Mom asks.

Mom's life mission is to make sure everybody's safe. That's why she works at the UN. She knows I'm fine with Dad and Alice. She's looking after the rest of the world.

"I just wonder who is looking after her?" Mom says again.

"The meanest lady in the world," I say, remembering the death look.

But Mom ignores what I say. "Whatever Carmeline is guilty of," she says, "this public shaming of a child —"

"But she's not guilty of anything," I say, interrupting her. "She wouldn't."

I know I'm right.

The next morning, as Vee, Jessie, and I walk past the hotel to our bus stop, we all **slow down** and try to look in the fancy front doors. I'm desperate to talk to Carmeline, and now I think she needs my help.

"I'm going to go meet her after school," I say.

"You can't," Jessie says. "They'll never let you in. Anyway, why would you want to meet someone like that?"

"Jessie, you're the one who always talks about evidence," I say. "What about **innocent until proven guilty?**"

Vee doesn't say anything, but I can tell she agrees with me. Vee and I both love Carmeline. **We loved her first.**

We cross at the traffic lights. The bus is coming slowly up the hill.

"What about those pictures in the paper?" Jessie says. "Aren't they proof?"

"They're proof that *someone* made the mess," I say. "Not that it was her."

"Well, who else?"

"The hotel staff?" suggests Vee.

"The Nanny could have done it," I say, even though I know she probably didn't. "Anyway. Someone needs to prove it wasn't Carmeline."

"And how are you going to do that?" Jessie asks.

I explain everything as we climb onto the bus.

"That's your plan?" Jessie asks. The bus wobbles to a start.

I nod.

"Just walk in and pretend we're staying there?" she repeats. "What kind of plan is that?"

Jessie **raises her eyebrows** at me. Vee **grins**.

"And once you're in, then what?" Jessie asks. "How do you know where to find her? Every grown-up in the hotel is going to know you're a fake in about one second."

"Well, do you have a better plan?" I ask, raising my eyebrows and grinning.

Chapter Five

By the end of the school day, Jessie and Vee have decided they're coming to meet Carmeline too. Jessie is still *saying* it's a terrible idea, but I know she secretly **can't resist an adventure.**

We decide school uniforms would be a dead giveaway, so we go home to get changed first. Baby is howling and arching out of Dad's arms. Dad's trying to get him into the sling, but Baby kicks his legs out of the holes faster than Dad can get them in.

"Can we go to the park?" I ask, pulling on Baby's toes. The park is half a block away. There are no roads to cross, so Dad and Alice usually let us go on our own if we ask.

Baby stops howling and reaches his fat little arms out to me. He snuggles his face into my neck. It's **soft** and **tickly**, and it makes me laugh. Baby giggles too. He's super cute.

"We'll take Baby," Jessie says, and I meet her eyes.

Brilliant. Grown-ups are way more likely to treat you with respect if you're carrying a baby.

Dad helps me strap Baby into the sling on my front. He tightens all the clips. Baby is pretty heavy, but he's still **gurgle-laughing**, and I like cuddling with him.

With Baby strapped on my front, we just **walk right through** the front doors of the hotel. The Fancy Men don't even blink at us. I pause in the lobby, feeling a little nervous. It's so much nicer than the lobby of our building. The lights are soft, and there are mirrors everywhere.

Jessie goes to the elevator and smiles at the woman waiting beside it. Vee and I follow. The woman **coos at Baby**. She swipes her card, and we get in behind her. She gets out on the second floor, so we do too. It's quiet and carpeted with no windows. Next to me there's a cart with lots of folded towels, little bars of soap, and plastic-wrapped cookies.

"**Now what?**" Vee whispers.

We stand there as the woman disappears through a door partway down the hall. We stare at each other. How are we going to find Carmeline Clancy in this building? **It's enormous.**

"Should we start knocking on all the doors?" I ask.

"Yeah, that's a great plan," Jessie says.

Vee starts to giggle. "Maybe we

should shout her name really loud," she suggests.

"Or go back down and steal a security card from one of the Fancy Men," I say.

All three of us crack up with laughter.

We stand there in the hall, laughing. **Baby gurgles and squeals** like he understands the joke.

The elevator dings behind us. We all spin around to see Carmeline Clancy's scary Nanny step out of the elevator.

She stares at us.

I glance sideways at Jessie and Vee. They both look really guilty.

"What's going on here?" the Nanny asks. She folds her arms and frowns at us. Then . . . **Carmeline Clancy steps out of the elevator behind her!**

"We came to meet Carmeline," I say, trying to sound brave, but my voice is really shaky.

"Oh, no you did not," says the Nanny.

"Hi," Carmeline says. "How's it going?" She reaches out to Jessie, who's the closest, and shakes her hand.

She sounds so nice and so much like she does on YouTube. I want to tell her how much I like her, but the Nanny doesn't even let me breathe in.

"Don't you even talk to her," she says. "I'm calling security to meet you at the elevator on first floor."

I'm so nervous that I squeeze Baby hard. He starts crying. I try to bounce him quiet, but he just gets louder.

"But —" Carmeline Clancy begins.

The Nanny stops her right there. "But nothing, miss. We are not having strangers **breaking into the hotel** on top of everything else."

Carmeline looks **sparklingly angry**, which is exactly how I feel. Baby is howling, and I can't think. In the middle of everything, I hear a dog barking down the hall and turn to look. But the Nanny is **bulldozing us into the elevator**.

We tumble into the lobby, and two Fancy Men are there to meet us. They take us by our elbows and lead us out the front doors of the hotel.

"You kids aren't allowed to play in here. Do you understand?" one of them says. He's talking to me like I'm in kindergarten. I wonder how long it will be before grown-ups stop baby-talking to me.

As we walk back to our own building, Baby finally calms down.

"We just met Carmeline Clancy," Jessie says like she doesn't quite believe it.

We reach our building. When we get in the elevator, Vee looks at Baby strapped to my chest. "Hey, what's he got?"

I look down. He has a plastic-wrapped cookie in his chubby hand. He must have grabbed it from the cart.

"Our Baby's a thief," Jessie says.

We all burst out laughing.

"Look out, Baby, that scary Nanny is gonna get you," Vee says in between laugh-snorts.

"Did anyone else hear a dog barking?" I say.

"No," Vee says, laughing harder.

"Carmeline seemed really nice, didn't she?" Jessie asks, getting serious again.

"Well, *yeah*," I say. I already knew she would be nice.

"We need to get to the bottom of this mess thing," Jessie says as the elevator opens into our hall.

Vee lets out a great **whooping** cheer. "What was that for?" I ask.

"Jessie just signed up."

"Signed up for what?" Jessie asks.

"**The Carmeline-Clancy-is-Innocent Mission,**" Vee says.

Chapter Six

The apartment smells like frying garlic, and Dad is standing by the stove. I unstrap Baby and put him on the rug on the kitchen floor by Dad's feet. We all collapse on the couch and talk quietly together so Dad can't hear.

"If Carmeline isn't responsible, then **someone's framing her**," Jessie whispers. "Otherwise why blame her?"

"Exactly," I say, and Vee nods.

"There are lots of people who could be framing her," says Jessie. "Let's make a list." Jessie loves making lists. She gets out her neat little notebook and writes:

- Hotel cleaners
- A jealous rock climber who wants to be the movie star
- The Fancy Men
- Other hotel guests

"The Nanny," I say.

"Squishy, the Nanny is looking after Carmeline. It can't be her," Vee says.

"But she's got the opportunity," I argue.

Jessie writes: The Nanny

"OK, what about motive?" Jessie asks. "What would the suspects get out of framing her?"

"Um, the hotel gets its picture on the news?" Vee suggests.

"Nanny gets to be more interesting," I say.

Trying to figure this out on a piece of paper is too hard. I just want to *do* something. I start doing **swoop-kicks** over the top of the couch and landing on the floor behind it. Vee laughs and does a **torpedo-roll** over the couch to land on top of me.

"Oof!" I say, and we both laugh.

"Guys," Jessie says. "We need to take this seriously!"

Vee's squashing my lungs so I can't talk right, but I say, "You know how . . . we take this . . . seriously?"

"How?" they ask.

I heave Vee off my back. "We signal Not-Boring Lady and tell her."

The others stare at me. I can see that **they're a little bit disappointed.**

"I know," I say. "It would be more fun to solve it ourselves. But this isn't just for fun. What about Carmeline Clancy? Somebody is ruining her life."

They agree but don't look happy.

Jessie digs out the signaling scarf Not-Boring Lady gave us. It's tucked under Jessie's rows of folded socks. **The scarf is enormous and red.** Vee climbs up onto the desk. She can't reach the curtain rod, so I stand next to the desk, and she puts one foot on my shoulder and holds onto the wall.

"Careful of the telescope," Jessie says.
"**Careful!**" The telescope is exactly
where Vee would land if she fell.

Vee dangles the scarf over
the curtain rod. It slips off.
She tries again.
It slips again.

Jessie goes to get binder clips.

"They're for my sheet music," she says, passing them up to Vee.

Vee clips the scarf to our curtains so it **hangs over our window**. The light in our bedroom turns a dark red, like sunset. Not-Boring Lady will know we need her when she sees it from her office.

"Dinner!" Dad calls.

Alice is working late tonight, so it's just us and Dad and Baby. I sit near Baby and spoon rice onto the table in front of him. **He's so funny**. He eats some, smears some on the table, and throws the rest on the floor. We're all laughing at him. He's laughing and slapping the table with his palms when **the door buzzes**.

We all look at each other in surprise. The door only buzzes when friends are coming, and usually we know they're on their way ahead of time.

Dad pushes back his chair and goes to the door speaker. "Hello? Oh, hello, yes. Yes, certainly. No, that's fine, we're sitting down to dinner, but if they signaled you? Yes, come on up. Eleventh floor."

Wow! Not-Boring Lady is not slow!

Dad looks a little amused and a little worried. "You kids signaled the Chief of Special Secret Undercover Operations?" he asks.

We nod.

"Whatever for?"

"Umm," I say. For some reason it feels a little embarrassing now, and I don't want to meet anybody's eyes.

Not-Boring Lady is at the door before we can explain anything. She's wearing a gray suit with a blue scarf tied neatly at her throat. Dad offers her Alice's chair, but she shakes her head. She stands next to the table, looking quickly into each of our faces.

"I saw the signal scarf," she says. "Do you need my help, girls?"

So the story about Carmeline Clancy tumbles out. We tell Not-Boring Lady how we think Carmeline is being framed, maybe by the Nanny, or maybe by the Fancy Men.

"**Fancy Men?**" Dad asks. We explain how Vee and I loved Carmeline Clancy first, how we're worried, and how we want to **prove she's innocent.**

Not-Boring Lady listens, but she starts shaking her head long before we're finished. We trail off.

"I would love to help you with your investigation, but this just isn't my area of expertise," she says.

"But what about Carmeline Clancy and her movie?" Vee asks.

"I'm sure the attention will die down in the next few days," says Not-Boring Lady. "She has a nanny. **She'll be fine.**"

Like *that* mean, scary lady is going to fix anything.

"I'm really sorry I can't help you girls with your mystery this time," Not-Boring Lady says. She truly does look sorry. "I can ask my colleagues for information. I'll let you know right away if I hear anything."

I see her **wink at Dad** before he walks her to the elevator, leaving us alone at the table.

"That's it," says Jessie. **"It's just us."**

We're going to have to prove Carmeline is innocent on our own.

Chapter Seven

"We need more information," Jessie says, rolling over in her bunk after lights out. Dad is being super-strict about our online time, so we can't Google anything. It makes Jessie **twitchy**.

"We need to know who is around," Jessie says. "And how they all feel about her."

"The criminal could be anyone," Vee says from the top bunk. She sounds kind of excited. "Could be a rival rock climber. Or a rival filmmaker."

It could be anyone.

"You know what we need to do?" I say. I sit up, because this is going to be fun. "We need to get close to her, so we can figure out what's going on."

"Like a stakeout," Vee says.

I can feel Jessie shaking her head. "A stakeout is for a place," she says. Jessie cares about how you use words. "We need to shadow her."

"Yeah," I say. **"Mission: shadow."**

"Starting tomorrow?" asks Vee.

"Right after school," says Jessie. "We'll go down to where they're filming."

Vee is so excited after school that she's almost jumping out the bus windows.

When we get home, Alice gets us granola bars for a snack. She tells us to go straight to the park and not to cross any roads. **We nod**. We're not going to the park, but a nod isn't a promise.

They're filming at one end of the street behind our building. There are rows of orange traffic cones, bright lights on tall stands, silver umbrellas, and at least **five enormous video cameras.** Three white trucks are parked at the other end. People with clipboards and lanyards are running around like they have to **save the world**. Others are standing around with cups of coffee, just talking.

There's a brand new fence blocking the way, and a small group of people are gathered along it, watching. You can tell that they have nothing to do with the film. They just want to be there and watch. They're a little bit like us, except **we're on a mission.**

We stand with them, our chests up to the fence, eating our granola bars and watching, but it's pretty boring. We're miles from Carmeline. We can hardly even see her, let alone hear what people say. There's no way we can find out who's framing her from here.

"We have to get closer," says Jessie.

I love Jessie. She's so responsible, but once she wants to know something, nothing gets in her way.

I can't see how we'll be able to get any closer, though. It's like a big desert of concrete between here and the filming. If we started to run across it, everyone would see.

Vee is on tiptoe trying to look.

I try to tell her it's hopeless. "You're not gonna see anything from here."

"I know, I know," she says. "But isn't that Not-John's grate?"

I stare down the side of the building. It is his grate!

One time, we met a runaway boy who said his name was John, but it wasn't. He lived in our parking garage and crawled in and out through a grate onto the sidewalk. His grate is right there in the middle of all the action.

"Vee, you are a genius," Jessie says.

We all turn and run, leaving the other watchers to the boringness. I smile. We're gonna be *so* much closer than they are.

Taking the stairs down to the parking garage is quicker than waiting for the elevator. We race down them. Lots of the parking spaces are empty — I guess because people like Alice are still at work.

Not-John's grate is above parking spot 503. He used to climb the hood of the car there, like a step to get in and out.

Right now there is no car. The grate is higher than our heads, but I can see feet going backward and forward up there.

There. **Those are Carmeline's.** I can tell by the **kid-sized feet** and the bright leggings. Those black trousers and **serious boots** next to her belong to the scary Nanny.

There's a pipe running along the wall at about knee height. I step onto it and grab for the grate. Then I pull up so my tummy is on the sill and my face is pushed against the bars. The old green porta-potty across the sidewalk is partly blocking my view.

Someone calls, **"Take seven!"** and the feet around me start walking away.

They head across the road to where the filming is taking place.

"What's happening?" Vee asks, trying to jump up beside me. There's not enough room for both of us.

"**Hang on,**" I say.

I shove the grate. It pops out, leaving a **Squishy Taylor-sized hole** to squeeze through.

Chapter Eight

I'm crouched behind the back of a movie truck, watching Vee struggle out of the grate hole. It's hard to get up there, and it's a tight **squeeze** to **shimmy** through.

There. She's out. She turns around to peer back into the garage.

I see Jessie's face pop up and then disappear, like she's jumping up to reach the grate. This is going to be hard for Jessie. She doesn't climb anything, ever.

Then Jessie's hand reaches up. Vee grabs it and tries to pull her out.

Jessie says, **"Ow! Ow! Stop!"** She rips her hand away from Vee's.

I glance around. We're partly hidden by the porta-potty and the movie truck, and luckily no one is watching us right now. I creep back to see if I can help. Jessie is down there in the dark, rubbing her hand, which looks sore.

"I don't think I can do it. You go without me," she says. "Just make sure you take note of all **suspicious activity.**"

I glance behind me. Carmeline is climbing partway up the building. There's a camera sliding up a long pole, following her as she goes. I desperately want to watch. I think about being selfless and trying to get Jessie out. But the filming is too fun to watch.

"OK," I say and leave her in the dark garage. I **creep along the side** of the truck, getting closer and closer to the set. Vee is right behind me. We **crouch in the shadow** of the truck to get a good look at what's going on.

Carmeline is at the seventh floor level now. It's really high. The camera is sliding alongside her at a slow, steady speed. I wish *I* was climbing the building with a camera beside me. The harness she's wearing is almost invisible. Her safety rope goes all the way up to the roof. There must be a rigging point up there.

I remember our mission. Who are all these people, and who is framing Carmeline? Could it be one of the camera operators? Where's the Nanny?

"Hey, you!" says a familiar voice. "I know you."

It's the Nanny. She's over by the cameras, and she's pointing directly at me. She looks really determined.

Vee sees her too and groans. "Oh, no."

The Nanny starts walking toward us, fast. We've got two options. Turn ourselves over or run.

We run.

I **dodge** around the side of the truck and under the leg of a big black tripod. There's a row of folding chairs. I **skid** around them and **bump** a table with doughnuts on it. Vee **pounds** after me. The Nanny is right behind her. I **knock** into a boy in an apron. "Oh, I'm sorry!" I say. He laughs as I **duck** away from him and keep running.

The Nanny shouts, "You kids, stop right now!"

I can hear people at the fence laughing at us. I **run** past a row of cameras. I **step** on a clipboard that's lying on the ground and **slide** on it like a skateboard. Then I **skid** off the clipboard and keep running.

I hear a familiar barking beside me. It's that puppy. He's got a big grin on his face, and **his tongue is dangling** out one side of his mouth. He's leaping around ridiculously at my feet, like I've just asked him to play a game. I want to pick him up and cuddle him, but there's no time.

I reach the building on the other side of the road, the one Carmeline Clancy is climbing. Except she's not climbing. She's quickly rappeling down it.

Vee and the Nanny are both trying to follow me. Then, all of a sudden, we're all tangled up together with a playful puppy.

Two paws leap up onto the Nanny's knees, and a big sloppy tongue tries to lick her hand.

"Bad dog," calls a voice. I turn and see Carmeline, running toward us, trailing her safety lines. Behind her, the cameras are in chaos.

A red-faced man is shouting, "Cut. Cut! Carmeline, what are you doing?"

"Bad dog," Carmeline says again.

The puppy doesn't think he's bad. He thinks the Nanny loves him. His tail is **wagging faster than a heartbeat.** The Nanny is totally distracted.

Now's our chance. I grab Vee's hand, and **we run at top speed** for the end of the alley. No one follows us.

Jessie meets us at the front door to our building. She looks scared but then sees we're OK. **She bursts out laughing.** We're breathing hard from so much running, but we laugh too. We slump against the lobby wall.

I'm kind of expecting someone from the movie set to turn up and tell Dad and Alice how bad *we* are.

What I'm not expecting is what's on the news when we get to the apartment.

Dad and Alice are putting out food on the table when it comes on. We're **sprawled on the floor**, trying to pretend everything is normal.

The announcer says, "*In breaking news, rock climbing movie star Carmeline Clancy has had her contract canceled this evening due to her behavior both on and off set. Controversy has dogged young Clancy since her arrival earlier this week.*"

There are some old shots of Carmeline rock climbing. Then they're showing the street **outside our building**. Luckily, Dad and Alice are talking loudly, not paying any attention, as the three of us lean in toward the TV.

There I am, **bolting under a tripod**, with Vee **racing along behind**. There's the Nanny running through the crowd. The puppy is knocking over chairs and slipping between cameras. The film set is **total chaos**.

"*Clancy's security guard is blaming some sneaky fans for today's events.*"

The Nanny comes on the screen.

I grab Vee's arm. "Oh, wow," I say. "That woman is a security guard. I *knew* she was **more than just a Nanny**."

The Nanny starts speaking. "*This afternoon's events were caused by some out-of-control fans who broke onto the set. People shouldn't blame Carmeline.*"

The reporter comes back on. "*Clancy continues to deny claims that she's caused thousands of dollars worth of damage to her hotel room over the past four nights. The young mess-maker has been confined to her hotel room until further notice."*

I sit back on my heels and look at my bonus sisters. Out-of-control fans. Confined to her hotel room. Carmeline isn't the only mess-maker.

Chapter Nine

"You know what this means," I say in bed that night.

"What?" Vee asks.

"**It's our fault** that Carmeline got fired," I say. "So now we really have to prove she's innocent."

I think about Mom's justice work she does for whole countries worth of people. Proving that **Carmeline**

Clancy is innocent feels like the least I can do.

"How will we do it?" asks Vee.

"Set up a **tiny video camera** in the hotel room?" suggests Jessie.

"Get a **tiny microphone** and clip it on the Nanny's coat," I say.

Vee and Jessie giggle and start making even funnier suggestions.

"Make **special X-ray glasses** that see through walls."

"Make a **truth spray** and spray it on the Fancy Men so that they tell."

We laugh so the bed shakes.

"Kids!" Dad calls. "We can hear you."

I pull the blanket up and shove the corner in my mouth to stop the laughs getting out.

When I've calmed down, I start to think about Carmeline locked in her hotel room. I think about how she doesn't have her mom, just a scary Nanny.

The next day is Friday, and we don't have a Carmeline Clancy Plan. All I know is **we have to do something.** At school, everyone is meaner about Carmeline than before. I try to think of a plan, but I can't.

When we get home, Baby is lying on the rug on the floor screaming while **Dad flaps around the kitchen.** He's made pizza dough, which is rising in a big bowl on the counter.

"There's no mozzarella," Dad says. He picks up Baby and bounces him on his hip. Dad tips the dough onto the counter and tries to knead it one-handed.

"I haven't even started making the sauce yet," Dad says. Baby cries even harder. He starts to **twist backward** out of Dad's arm. Dad grabs him with his flour-covered hand.

"Do you want us to take Baby and go get some mozzarella?" I ask.

Dad gives me a **floury kiss** on the top of my head. "Squishy, that would be amazing. My wallet is in my coat pocket."

Vee helps strap Baby onto my front. I jiggle him and nuzzle his cheek with my nose while Jessie grabs a shopping bag.

Baby hiccups and snorts a little. Then he stops crying.

"See you soon, kids!" Dad calls, and he closes the door behind us.

The store is on the far corner, just past Carmeline's hotel. We just hang around near the tree, watching the Fancy Men.

Baby has my hair in both fists and is pulling hard. I start untangling his fingers, using it as an excuse to stop outside the hotel. The others stop beside me.

"Hey, look!" Vee says, pointing.

Carmeline Clancy opens a window on the second floor. We're so close, almost underneath her. She leans out, looks at the tree branch beside her, and then ducks back inside. **But not for long.**

Another shape fills the window. I'm confused at first. What does she have? It's **gray and squirming.** Then I recognize it. Carmeline is holding the puppy!

"What is she *doing*?" Vee asks.

"Holding the puppy out the window," says Jessie.

"No way, really?" I say, watching the wriggling dog scrabble on the big tree branch. He doesn't look happy, even though Carmeline is very gentle. She makes sure he's balanced on a big branch and talks to him quietly.

Then she glances down between the leaves and sees us.

"Are you all right?" I ask. I cannot believe I actually just spoke to Carmeline Clancy!

She kind of nods her head, but says, "It's just about Messy."

"Messy?" I ask, and then I realize Messy is the puppy's name.

"They'll take him to the pound," Carmeline says. She sounds like she's trying not to cry.

I think about the time our class at school visited the pound. Remembering all those sad-looking dogs and cats in cages makes me feel like crying too.

Messy is all trembly, crouching close to the branch. He looks scared.

"He's a stray," Carmeline explains. "I found him when I first got here, and I've been taking care of him."

All my sightings of the puppy finally make some sense.

"Why are you putting him in the tree?" Jessie asks before I can.

Carmeline Clancy half-grins, but she looks worried too. "I've been sneaking him in and out through a side door, but now I'm locked in."

She looks as though she's about to follow the dog out the window, but then she's startled by a noise in the room behind her.

Carmeline Clancy leans down with a frightened face. "They're coming!" she says. "Look after Messy." She slams the window shut and spins her back to it.

Carmeline Clancy has given us a mission, and we can't let her down.

"Do you think Carmeline's going to be OK?" Jessie asks.

If she's not, it's our fault.

Messy starts to make barky, whiny little dog noises.

"We need to save the puppy," I say, trying to untangle Baby's fingers from my hair again.

Jessie springs into action. "I'll try and get to Carmeline. Vee, you get the puppy," she says, then looks at me. "You look after Baby."

Now I wish I didn't have Baby, but there's no time to swap.

Jessie **bolts past the Fancy Men** into the hotel. They shout and chase her inside, which is probably good because otherwise they'd be watching Vee.

Vee is scrambling up the tree. Her fingers dig into little spaces in the rough bark. **She's like a spider-ninja.**

I stare upward as Vee gets higher and higher, wishing it was me.

When Vee reaches Messy's branch, she stands up and walks along it, one hand on the hotel wall for balance. She offers Messy her knuckles to sniff. He reaches out with his nose and lets Vee scratch him behind the ears. It's **extra-cute** and makes me feel jealous.

Vee lifts him up against her hip. Amazingly, he doesn't seem to mind. He knows we're going to look after him. Vee carries him carefully back to the trunk.

Her face goes pale as she looks toward the ground, and I realize what the problem is.

There's no way she can climb down with the puppy under her arm.

Chapter Ten

"Hang on, Vee! I'm coming up," I call. I unclip Baby's sling from my front and shrug my shoulders out of it.

"You can't leave Baby on the ground!" Vee shouts.

"I know," I say. I've got a plan. I keep Baby close and **turn the sling** around so he's on my back. He kicks his **fat little legs and wiggles**. It's awkward getting his head under my armpit, but

I finally get the sling onto my back and pull the straps **extra tight**.

Vee is straddling the branch like it's a pony, with her knees gripping tight. Messy is huddled up next to the tree trunk, whining and shivering.

I double-check and triple-check to make sure Baby's straps are secure.

"You OK, Baby?" I ask. He's got his hands in the back of my hair, pulling handfuls and giggling like crazy. I start to climb.

It's hard. Baby is heavy, and I'm not as good a climber as Vee. My fingers hurt as I grip the bark. Once I get to the first branch, it's better. I grab it with both hands and swing one leg over. It's like **monkey bars, only bigger.** I scramble to my feet on the branch, holding on tight to the trunk.

I start thinking about Baby on my back. He might be chubby, but he suddenly feels **small and breakable**. I pull myself up to the next branch, even more carefully than before. If I fall, Baby falls with me. Finally I'm standing on the branch underneath Vee and Messy.

"Now what?" asks Vee.

I stare up at her. We're two stories up, with a Baby and a Messy. This is as far as my plan went.

"Pass him down to me?" I suggest.

Vee, still gripping the branch with her knees, lifts Messy around the chest. As she lifts him, Messy stretches out. His tummy is bare and pink, and his legs seem very long. He looks **so funny** that I would laugh, but I'm too scared for Baby.

I lean my shoulder against the tree trunk, bracing my feet to make them strong, and **reach up for Messy**.

"Here, boy. You're all right. Good dog," I say. He's so soft. I hold him close, burying my fingers in his fur, feeling his frightened trembling.

"Nice work," says Vee, swinging down to join us. She **climb-slides down** to the next branch, and I pass Messy down to her.

We can do this. It's easy. We take turns lifting the **terrified puppy** down to each other. Baby feels warm against my back and the difference in my balance

is starting to feel normal. The lower we get, the less scary it is. I cling to the last branch while **Vee jumps to the ground.**

I lower Messy toward Vee. This last section of trunk without branches is longer than all the others, and Vee's arms are too short. The puppy half-falls onto her, knocking her over. She lands on her knees with a thump. **"OW!"** she says.

The fall startles me, and my foot slips. I reach for the trunk, but it's not where I thought. My hand scrapes down the bark, and I **thump** onto my tummy on the branch. I grab at anything, trying to hold on. My foot slides into thin air.

Baby! I can't land on Baby.

I don't know which way is up. My hands and legs are flapping. My chin is jammed against the tree bark. Baby is crying, Messy is barking, and Vee is saying, **"Squishy, hold on!"**

I've slid around so I'm under the branch. I'm holding on with my arms and legs, like a **terrified sloth.**

"What are you kids doing?"

It's the Fancy Men running out through the hotel doors.

Chapter Eleven

My first thought is to let go and drop to the ground, because I don't want to be rescued by **puppy-haters**.

But I can't let Baby get hurt.

Fine. The mean grown-ups can help me down. I cling on, my arms trembling as the Fancy Men run toward us. I have to **keep Baby safe**.

But the men don't make it to us.

It turns out that Messy, who was terrified of heights, is not terrified of the Fancy Men. The dog plants himself in their path and starts to growl. All the hair around his shoulders stands up like spikes.

"Yikes!" says one of the Fancy Men, and they slow down.

It gives me the minute I need. I say, "It's OK, Baby. It's going to be OK."

I let go with my legs and swing from my arms. I'm too far from the main trunk, so I have to move hand over hand toward it. It's hard. Baby is so heavy, and the rough bark hurts my hands, but we make it to the trunk. I grab it and half-hold on, half-slide down it. Vee reaches up and slows me down.

I land on both feet. Vee holds on to my shoulders and stops me and Baby from falling over backward.

When I turn around, one of the Fancy Men has a phone to his ear. Messy is still growling at him.

"Is this the animal police?" the man says.

"No!" I shout, but before I can say anything else, Carmeline Clancy runs out of the hotel with Jessie beside her.

"You will *not* call the pound," Carmeline Clancy says to the man. He stares at her and lowers his cell phone from his ear. Messy runs to her, nuzzling his head against her leg. Carmeline Clancy turns to me. **"Nice climbing,"** she says.

I'm breathing hard. My hands are bleeding, and my T-shirt is torn. But Baby is safe, and Carmeline Clancy just said, "**Nice climbing.**" To *me*. Vee nudges me with her elbow. Jessie winks.

"We saw a couple of your moves from the window," Carmeline says, nodding up toward her room. "Cute baby," she adds and comes over to grab Baby's waving hand.

"**Carmeline!**" a voice calls. It's the scary Nanny, coming out of the hotel. "What are you doing out of your room?"

Carmeline turns to her. "I had to save the puppy," she says.

Messy still thinks the Nanny is his best friend. He **gallops** over to her and tries to **kiss** her knees. The Nanny actually smiles and suddenly looks a lot less scary.

Carmeline laughs. "Messy! Stop it. Bad dog."

The Nanny looks up at Carmeline. I can see her face change as she connects the dots. "Messy?" she asks. "Messy? You've been hiding a dog in your hotel room? That's what this whole mess thing has been about?"

Carmeline looks embarrassed. "They were going to take him to the pound. I didn't know what to do."

"Well, you could have told me!" the Nanny explodes. "Then *I* could have done something about it! How can I look after you if you don't tell me what's going on?"

I glare at the Nanny. I can't stop myself from speaking. "Well, you should be **less scary**," I say. "Then she might tell you things."

The Nanny looks stunned.

One of the Fancy Men steps forward. "I'm sorry, miss, but you cannot keep a puppy in the hotel. I'm afraid I will have to **call the pound**."

There's a silence. I'm thinking fast. The puppy needs a home right now.

"It's OK," I say. "We'll take him."

Jessie and Vee both look at me like I'm crazy. Maybe I am, but I don't care. I pat my knee. "Come on, boy."

Messy **jump-hop-runs** to me with his big brown eyes and his sweet, **tongue-drooping grin**. I reach down to scratch the soft fur behind his ears and feel a big heartbeat of love.

But then I look up. Carmeline Clancy seems sad and a little lonely. I feel guilty, even though I just saved her dog. I don't know what to say.

"Do you want to come to our place for dinner in an hour?" Jessie asks her. "Tom's making pizza."

When we come home with the mozzarella and Messy the dog, Dad and Alice look as though we just brought a dinosaur into the house.

"What is that?" Dad asks, as if he can't tell it's a puppy.

"It's a puppy," I say. Then I add, "We're keeping him."

"No, we are not," Dad and Alice say at the same time.

Messy starts **dog-speed-racing** around the family room. He discovers a dangerous **couch-cushion enemy** and attacks it. He growls and bites, shaking it hard so his ears flop from side to side. White stuffing flies everywhere.

I remember the pictures of Carmeline Clancy's **destroyed hotel room**. It makes a lot of sense now.

I grab Messy and pull him onto my knee, scratching his tummy and making him wriggle and wag his tail. He turns around and starts to lick my face.

Dad and Alice are talking about calling the pound.

Jessie turns on **the TV news**. There's something bad happening on the other side of the world. And then Carmeline Clancy's face is on the screen.

"I'm so glad the movie is going ahead," she says. "I apologized to the director, and he forgave me. I also apologized to the hotel manager. He agreed to let me stay until filming is over."

"Is it true," the reporter asks, "that you won't say how your hotel room was destroyed?"

"I'll only say I was protecting someone," Carmeline says. **"It was a matter of life or death."**

Messy squirm-wiggles out of my arms and leaps toward the TV, almost knocking it over to try to get through the screen to Carmeline.

Chapter Twelve

Carmeline Clancy is sitting right next to me in my apartment eating pizza. **I'm so happy I can't breathe.** I'm feeding pepperoni to Messy under the table. Carmeline is putting little pieces of crust in front of Baby, who thinks she's the **best thing ever.** I agree with him.

Dad and Alice are talking quietly with the Nanny.

"I can't believe she let it happen," the Nanny says.

Carmeline turns around. "They were going to take him to the dog pound," she says. Dad and Alice have on their best understanding-faces.

Carmeline keeps talking. "The first morning I got here, people from the dog pound came, but I hid him. I tried to keep him from wrecking my room, but I couldn't stay awake all night."

Dad and Alice smile, but the Nanny is serious. "Well, Carmeline, this family can't keep him."

I look at Dad and Alice, who are shaking their heads. I'm suddenly desperate. "But . . ." I say. "Please."

"I guess we'll need to go with Plan B," Carmeline says, turning to me. "I found a puppy school where he can stay while I'm filming. Afterward, I'll take him home to Colorado."

I nod, feeling a little empty. But Carmeline is still talking. She's smiling at Vee and Jessie too. "I'm wondering if **you can help me**," she says. "I need someone to bring Messy to visit me every day while I'm filming. Could you guys do that?"

She wants us to visit her every day while she's filming?

I scream. Vee cheers so loudly it scares Messy. He starts barking under the table. Baby starts to cry, but then he stops and starts laughing.

"Messy's licking his toes!" Carmeline says. We all duck our heads under the table to watch.

Baby's little pink toes are curling and kicking, and Carmeline Clancy is laughing right beside me.

About the Author and Illustrator

Ailsa Wild is an acrobat, whip-cracker, and teaching artist who ran away from the circus to become a writer. She taught Squishy all her best bunk-bed tricks.

Ben Wood started drawing when he was Baby's age and happily drew all over his mom and dad's walls! Since then, he has never stopped drawing. He has an identical twin, and they used to play all kinds of pranks on their younger brother.

Author Acknowledgements

Christy and Luke, for writing residencies, bunk-bed acrobatics, and the day you turned the truck around.

Antoni, Penni, Moreno, and the masterclass crew, for showing me what the journey could be. Here's to epiphanies.

Indira and Devika, because she couldn't be real without you.

Hilary, Marisa, Penny, Sarah, and the HGE team, for making it happen. What an amazing net to have landed in.

Ben, for bringing them all to life.

Jono, for independence and supporting each other's dreams.

— Ailsa

Illustrator
Acknowledgements

Hilary, Marisa, Sarah, and the HGE team,
for your enthusiasm and spark.

Penny, for being the best! Thanks for
inviting me along on this Squish-tastic ride!
(And for putting up with all my emails!)

Ailsa, for creating such a fun place for
me to play in.

John, for listening to me ramble on and
on about Squishy Taylor every day.

— Ben

Talk About It!

1. Squishy is serious about helping people — and animals. Why do you think helping is important to her? What are ways you can be helpful to others?

2. Squishy's mom says that the news reporter is shaming Carmeline Clancy. Do you think this is true? In what ways was Carmeline shamed?

3. In this story, Squishy and her bonus sisters break the rules several times in order to help Carmeline Clancy. Name some of the rules they broke. Do you think it's OK to break some rules to help people?

Write About It!

1. Squishy puts herself and Baby in danger to help Carmeline Clancy. Write about a safer option Squishy could have chosen to help.

2. Squishy, Vee, and Jessie look up to Carmeline. Is there a movie or sports star you admire? Write a story about meeting him or her. What would you say or ask?

3. The girls believe that Carmeline Clancy didn't ruin her hotel room. What proof do they have that Carmeline is innocent? Write about a time when you had to prove you were right to a grown-up.